CHRISTMAS COMES TO MONSTER MOUNTAIN

Story by
John Barrett

Illustrations by
Rick Reinert Productions

Developed by
The LeFave Company

Ideals Publishing Corp.

Milwaukee, Wisconsin

ISBN 0-8249-8024-7

$\mathcal{T}$his story might seem unbelievable. But Ted E. Bear claims it really happened. As proof that the story is true, Teddy donated his reindeer bell and North Pole flight map to the Bearbank County Museum.

Ted's story began on Monster Mountain, just a few days before Christmas. Monster Mountain is where all the world's monsters live . . . when they are not out doing monsterous things.

Count Dracula, the leader of the monsters, was running for reelection. "If I do something really rotten," he said, "I will be reelected by a landslide!"

"Right, boss," said his secretary, Miss Witch. "Monsters appreciate rotten things."

Dracula grinned. "I know! I will kidnap Santa Claus!"

Miss Witch whistled. "That is really rotten!"

"We will need anti-reindeer missiles," said Miss Witch.

"Not at all," cackled Dracula. "I will simply write a letter to Santa Claus. When he brings my present, we will catch him in a Santa-trap!"

Miss Witch smiled. "When you're reelected, the whole world will be an uglier place, boss."

Dracula giggled an evil giggle and wrote:

DEAR SANTA:
  I HAVE BEEN A ~~BAD~~ GOOD BOY ALL YEAR. PLEASE BRING ME A SPIDER.   LOVE,
      LITTLE DRACULA

On Christmas Eve, Santa Claus slid down Dracula's chimney and was instantly caught in a stoutly built Santa-trap. "I have put an end to Christmas," laughed Dracula. "When the monsters see what I have done, I will get every vote on Monster Mountain."

Santa's reindeer waited on the roof. When Santa Claus did not return, they began to worry. Finally, they flew off for help.

The closest city to Monster Mountain was Bearbank. It was an unlikely place to find help because bears usually sleep all winter. Luckily, one little bear was awake. Ted E. Bear was watching the late show when he heard sleigh bells outside his apartment. He looked at his clock. "A quarter to January," he exclaimed. "I wonder who's out there?"

Teddy dashed outdoors. He saw Santa's sleigh and reindeer . . . but no Santa Claus.

Teddy Bear looked in the sleigh. There was Santa's Christmas list. The first name on the list was Count Dracula. "Oh oh," said Teddy. "Those monsters are up to something."

Teddy was worried. He would have to help. But how could he? He had never flown a bear-plane, let alone a big sleigh. "If Santa needs help, I'd better try," said the little bear.

After a bumpy takeoff roll, Ted was on his way.

Count Dracula had placed Santa Claus on display in front of Madison Scare Garden. Monsters from all over the mountain were gathering to see Santa.

As Teddy flew over, he heard Count Dracula giving his reelection speech: "Vote for me! I have captured Santa Claus! There will be no more Christmas for the world!"

"Oh no!" thought Teddy. "What am I going to do?"

If he landed the sleigh, he would surely be captured by the monsters. But if Santa Claus wasn't rescued, there would be no Christmas . . . or would there? He glanced about the sleigh. There was Santa's Christmas list and his flight map.

"I'll deliver the presents myself," said Teddy. "Those monsters might stop Santa, but they won't stop Christmas!"

Ted E. Bear went to work.

He flew from city to city. He jumped into chimneys with sacks full of presents. He found milk and cookies in almost every home. He ate as many cookies as a little bear could.

Soot from thousands of chimneys turned Ted E. Bear into a little ball of black dirt. "How does Santa Claus keep his suit clean?" he wondered.

Teddy finished and flew back to Monster Mountain just as Christmas Day was dawning. There were presents left over (Santa always takes extras) so Teddy placed them in the homes of little goblins and ghouls. He left presents for all sorts of monsterous creatures. He even left a new broom for Miss Witch.

Then he drove the sleigh to the alley behind Madison Scare Garden.

Ted E. Bear walked right into the crowd of monsters!

"*I* have put an end to Christmas!" Dracula was shouting.

"No, you haven't," said Teddy. Surprised, everyone turned to look at the sooty little bear. "Christmas will continue even if Santa is locked in your trap," Ted continued.

Dracula looked around. Little ghouls and goblins began to appear carrying beautifully decorated packages. A ghost wore a brand new sheet. Mummies displayed new wrappings.

"I think that dirty little bear is right, boss," said Miss Witch. She smiled as she held up a beautiful new broom.

"Then I haven't stopped Christmas?" moaned Dracula. "This is politically embarrassing. I'll lose the election."

"You won't lose the election," said Ted E. Bear. "Look! The monsters are happy!"

"That's strange," said Dracula. "Nobody's ever been happy on Monster Mountain."

Teddy smiled. "That's what Christmas does," he said. "It makes everybody happy. You'll get a lot more votes if you let Santa Claus out of that cage."

Count Dracula unlocked the Santa trap. The monsters cheered.

"Vote for Dracula!" shouted Miss Witch. "He brought Christmas to Monster Mountain!"

$\mathcal{T}$eddy, Santa Claus, Dracula, and the monsters had a big Christmas party. Santa promised to come back next year if the monsters were very good.

Before he left, Santa took Teddy to his sleigh. "You gave away all the presents," he said. "There's nothing left for you."

"That's all right," said Ted E. Bear.

"No, it isn't," said Santa Claus. He walked to his team of reindeer and plucked a silver bell from Blitzen's harness. "Here," said Santa. "And take this flight map just in case you have to help again." He handed Teddy a North Pole flight map.